LOUISE DIPS
THE PREDATO

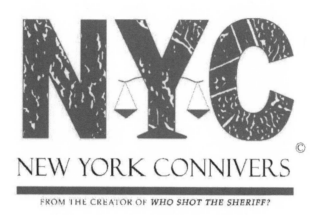

N·Y·C ©
NEW YORK CONNIVERS

FROM THE CREATOR OF *WHO SHOT THE SHERIFF?*

International Bestselling Author
John A. Andrews

Published in the U.S.A. by
Books That Will Enhance Your Life™

A L I - Andrews Leadership International
Entertainment Division®
Jon Jef Jam Entertainment®
www.JohnAAndrews.com

Cover Design: John A. Andrews
Cover Graphic Designer: A L I
Edited by:A L I
ISBN: 9798607901608

LOUISE DIPSON
THE PREDATOR

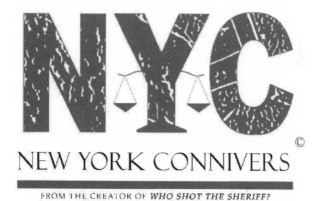

NEW YORK CONNIVERS ©

FROM THE CREATOR OF *WHO SHOT THE SHERIFF?*

THE PREQUEL

TABLE OF CONTENTS

1

Sirens crescendo throughout Williamsburg, New York. This close-knit commune cliff-hanging the Boroughs of Queens, Manhattan, and Brooklyn reverberate with the noise of calamitic proportions. Setting that populous on edge.

The McDonalds' parking lot now the focal point of the calamity is inundated with Sheriff cars, NYPD cruisers, and artillery. Mixed with the cries of neighbors, patrons, and friends the people cluster in multiple animated huddles. Some swearing. Some disorganized. Some dumbfounded. Others totally discombobulated. Pow-wows cut like a two-edged sword.

"She just left the house to grab a six-piece Chicken McNuggets, French fries and a soda. That's all. Now she's missing...gone. I can't believe someone did this to Deslyn. She never bothered anyone."

Says her mother Dorothy mortified with tearful eyes and slippery cheeks.

"Whoever did this to our little Maddy will pay the consequence. Why did it take the police so long to get here? They could have prevented this...They are never on time when you really need them."

Shadow the other parent Alecia Soprano. Also, in tears and showing photos of Deslyn on a busted screen iPhone with one hand and waving the other aerially seeking justice and empathy.

Meanwhile, in that now merging former huddle, Maddy's mother is engrossed in conversation with Detective Jonathan Hobbs and Detective Jamie Johnson states:

"She doesn't do any drugs...None at all! Why? What are you implying? Who is behind this...?"

In the meantime, friends, and neighbors, in yet another cluster share their concerns.

"They were only thirteen and fourteen years old."
Voiced another rattled neighbor as she paces back and forth and then circles multiple huddled acquaintances. While holding on tightly to the hand of her young teen daughter.

Other frantic teens converge. Some chaperoned, some unsupervised, others unleashed. Seemingly, the leader in that pack, a tall and slender girl with amber green hair and displaying her total independence with hand gestures. She chimes in verbally:

"Dessie and Maddy are my BFF's...Totally for life! They never got into any trouble. Why did someone have to do such injustice? Why did anyone...? Why? Please, somebody, help me understand. This is an unlawful act not only my friends but on our community. That's why I'll be attending law school after I graduate Williamsburg High! The Senate is falling asleep at their posts. It's time to get these predators off our streets. I shall! I must!"

Detectives Hobbs and Johnson are now engaged in the questioning of a uniformed green-bloused-khaki-pants McDonald's employee. She walks out of the restaurant terrified and still trembling like a leaf. Her name tag reads Arlene Gomez – Shift Manager.

"Yes. The two girls after being served walked out of the restaurant. First, they contemplated eating in. One of them said it's way too hot and congested inside this joint. And then they bounced...I mean, they headed out the door. They were glued to their smartphones, texting like crazy."

"Who served them?"

Asked Det. Johnson.

"It was I. I did…They were acting weird. One said she wanted chocolate shake then changed her mind to vanilla after being served."

Said the Shift Manager.

Meanwhile, additional Law Enforcement in marked and unmarked vehicles arrive in droves. Even some ambulances join their convoys. The two lead detectives Hobbs and Johnson press alertly for answers to these missing teens dilemma. It was clear to them the only eyewitness was Arlene Gomez.

Multiple parents, some seemingly preoccupied with their after-work chores bear down, reacting to the news.

"Shortly after they came outside." The Manager continued… "In a flash, a midnight blue SUV pulled up. The front door opened. They were thrown inside through the rear door. The vehicle took off speedily. That's all I saw. OMG! Why did this have to happen on my watch?"

She stated, still trembling.

"Did you get a glimpse of the license tags or the driver, anybody?"

Asked Detective Hobbs still drilling Arlene Gomez.

"No. I did not. Everything seemed to happen so fast like a scene from a Spider-Man movie. By the time it registered, the vehicle sped away leaving smoke and the sound of squealing tires in our parking lot. Just like that, it was gone. Gone through those back streets."

Detective Johnson radios:

"A Midnight blue SUV, over! With freshly peeled tires. Make and model unidentified!"

Multiple once parked police vehicles abandon the parking lot in haste and careens through increasing gridlocked street traffic.

Meanwhile, several onlookers continually vent:

"She knows who did it. This is such a cover-up!"

Pointing to the fast-food outlet.

2

With the getaway fresh in the air. Law Enforcement pounced in warlike demeanor. They set up roadblocks along major streets throughout Williamsburg, stretching across the bridge to Delancey Street and extended towards the Holland Tunnel and on selective Manhattan streets.

Also, strategically within the Five Boroughs. Ultimately, they concentrated a heavy police presence on the viaducts leading up to the Lincoln Tunnel and George Washington Bridge on the New York City sides.

Secondly, the Verrazano Bridge connecting Brooklyn with Staten Island was targeted as yet another checkpoint.

Thirdly, they sat up checkpoints at the entrances to both John F. Kennedy and La Guardia airports.

Discussion among the lead detectives mounted in the case. Hobbs and Johnson announced their concerns surrounding that Staten Island and through New Jersey pass.

Consequently, the Belt parkway East and West suffered tremendous traffic gridlock along with major streets flowing into this shoreline parkway wrapping around the coastal portion of Brooklyn.

The traffic alerts sent to New Yorkers cell phones read "Very strong police presence around the Belt Parkway East and West of the Verrazano Bridge. Avoid it at all costs."

The New York Mayor made some subsequent remarks urging New Yorkers to avoid certain gridlock traffic routes and if they see something, please say something. In addition to these checkpoints at major New York airports, a strong National Guard presence complimented. They were destined toward trapping this predator.

Meanwhile, multiple SUV's painted midnight blue became under vicious scrutiny. Many motorists driving identifying utility vehicles were pulled over, questioned and vehicles searched. While these motorists underwent such inquiry, some of the questions raised to them included:

"Where are you heading to?

Have you been through Williamsburg in the last ten hours?"

Displaying signs detailing profiles of the victims:

"Have you seen these two girls in the last ten hours?

Have you seen another SUV in this same color subverting traffic?" All those questions mounted as Mt. Everest within the investigation.

Law Enforcement understood though: typically, anyone with an SUV that color would normally detect one similar even though not in the same make and model. Anything to connect the dots. It was universally understood motorists are conditioned to detect other autos in their league.

The Newsflash on Cable TV stations as well as Network TV and even Radio, sounded like a broken record throughout that Friday night's already scheduled programs and continuing into early Saturday morning newscasts: *If you see a suspicious* *midnight blue SUV. Please say something by calling the NYPD immediately. **800-577-TIPS**.*

3

With limited information on the identity of this runaway predator. Law enforcement was caught handicapped in their expedition. Bringing in the suspect seemed like a mountainous climb without corroborating imagery or even a criminal backstory. Even so, they were determined to find answers. Any SUV which looked like or smelled like the getaway vehicle, uniformed police pulled over in their quest to solve this criminal outrage.

At the stroke of midnight on Saturday, a little over 24 hours since Maddy St. Hilaire and Deslyn Soprano disappeared from the Williamsburg neighborhood, NYPD officers pulled over and searched many suspicious SUVs. In particular, one along the Bronx River Parkway, bolting towards the George Washington Bridge.

Inside this vehicle, they discovered and seized multiple rifles along with other ammunition. That motorist was also questioned and detained. This motorist claimed he worked with the New York Corrections and was transporting weapons to Rikers. When pressed for his badge and ID, he claimed he rushed out of the house forgetting them. They slapped cuffs on him and later impounded the vehicle.

By early morning, Sunday his vehicle was swept. It turned up clean of any of the girl's DNA. Reportedly, calls came in from the correction department: their driver was returning to base at Rikers after a seizure. Even though he was ID by those officers. They were not leaving anything up to chance.

Their quest to catch this predator before he or she struck again like a sore wound was fermenting and smelled - urgent.

A short time thereafter, additional news in the case surfaced. Arlene Gomez, the McDonald's employee was further questioned by Hobbs and Johnson at the precinct.

"The Predator was fully masked who pulled off the abduction of those two teenagers."

Arlene Gomez recalled.

Subsequently, that McDonald's fast food restaurant surveillance camera was played back. Ironically, there was no surveillance footage to support the crime. "Very odd!" complained Detective Johnson. All that non-information, thrown into the mix consequently presented a severe challenge for this investigation with this predator still at large.

Meanwhile, fingers still pointed at Arlene Gomez. Not only in the media but also in the Williamsburg community. "Did she have anything to do with the crime? Was she complicit? Was she a cover-up in this abduction?" were some of the concerns raised.

Subsequently, Arlene Gomez was arrested on suspicion charges of this twin abduction of young teen girls.

4

As a result of Friday night's tragedy, parents began reigning in their young teens-girls by 7:00 PM. On Monday night, exactly three nights after the Williamsburg hit. Bedford-Stuyvesant, Brooklyn was also victimized. The third girl in this abduction string was nabbed.

Marlene Monroe, a fifteen-year-old girl was snatched outside the Fulton Street and Nostrand Avenue Mall. Onlookers described what they witnessed during that lightning speed abduction: *Someone with moves like a woman and masked fleeing the street in mint green Land Rover.*

After corroborating statements made by an onlooker, who once again was unable to capture the vehicle's temporary tags. It seemed like the same scenario explained to the lead detectives. In an interview with CNN, Detectives Hobbs and Johnson begged to differ. "Copycats don't act like that. This is too dangerous a crime for someone fearing such incriminating scrutiny by the 'red alerted' NYPD to emulate. This by far seems like the actions of a sole proprietor."

Said the flustered detective Jamie Johnson.

Now on high alert, the NYPD dispatched convoys from their fleet throughout Bedford-Stuyvesant and other neighboring communities. While some still claimed it was a copycat incident, Hobbs and Johnson weren't sharing those sentiments. They pressed the entire NYPD department for assistance. It did not only escalate with those two cops' pursuit but the parents of now all three teens pressured their neighbors to write their senators and congressmen for help in capturing this minuscule yet, insufficiently unidentified predator.

Some news reporting legal scholars reasoned:

"Now that another similar or related incident has occurred. Copycat or not. Law enforcement could be placed in a state of confusion. Not only are they in search of a midnight blue SUV without identifiable license tags but they are also looking for a mint-green Land Rover with unidentifiable tags. Plus, there is very little info on the identity of the predator. What role is the DMV playing in all of this?"

In response, Law enforcement claimed their street cameras might finally turn up images of any of those two vehicles. Plus, any other abductions could be hindered.

"They need to update those cameras. They are probably outdated. Thus, only good at catching motorists who run the red light. That's all."

Said a concerned Williamsburg parent.

Meanwhile, Arlene Gomez, the shift manager at that McDonalds in Williamsburg was released from police custody. Law enforcement realized the abduction spree was very much still alive while Gomez sat.

5

It has now been more than a week since the first abduction occurred inside that McDonald's parking lot. Yet, at this point, no arrests were made. With the identity of the predator still unmasked. Several entities close to the case remained on edge hoping they could easily slice into this pent-up case.

While the search was concentrated in NYC and those connecting cities toward New Jersey, the FBI embarked on a nation-wide search. Most airports were heavily armed now even Newark Airport in New Jersey and Bradley International in Connecticut with attack dogs, assault weaponry State Troopers, the military, and even the Army's National Guards. In a sense, it was metaphorically going to war domestically versus that predator like none before.

In the meantime, up and down the Hudson River police helicopters and speedboats roamed.

"Whoever started this was going to pay."

Said Hobbs lead detective on the case to a low-level officer and echoing the wish of New York's Mayor.

On the other hand, many other cops low on the totem pole and inundated with constant street patrol showed much frustration in body language and attitude.

LATER, at a gas station in White Plains, a midnight blue SUV in question pulled up to refuel. The station attendant in her twenties but looking like eighteen to look younger, instinctively reached for the phone and began dialing.

She dialed 91 before aborting the call as the driver attired NYPD uniformed walked inside, lay a $100 bill on the counter and said:

"I need a full tank on pump number nine."

The attendant still rattled but much less than when the vehicle pulled up alongside the pump and that motorist put that crisp *Franklin* on the counter. She quickly dispatched the note in her draw and nervously entertained the other customer in the line. The attendant remained puzzled. "Is this a man or a woman?" She questioned under her breath.

Meanwhile, the motorist sauntered towards the pump island. At pump number nine, the motorist pumped almost $95.00 in the vehicle's empty tank and kept on pumping until the entire $100 worth was consumed. Returning to the driver's seat a brawl broke out with one of the passengers. Madly, the driver dispenses a sharp upper-cut followed by a left jab on the attacker. Screams erupted with different tempos. With the driver's window half-cocked, the attacker a teen girl chilled. The eavesdropping attendant peripherally witnessed and overheard those excruciating altercations to the opponent's head.

Immediately, the attendant grabbed the telephone receiver, reached into her drawer and scanned the $100 dollar bill. Realizing it was fake, she instantly dialed 911.

By this time the vehicle had already speedily departed the gas station. Westchester County police arrived minutes later but there was no one to buttonhole. Multiple $25,000.00 rewards signs plastered NYC.

6

The predator had now for the first time left some bread crumbs for the ravens who were aggressively tailing. The gas station attendant told them everything she overheard and witnessed. So, as the news spread like a California brush fire with nationwide proportions, law enforcement was busily putting the pieces together all evening and night long to come up with a plausible strategy for their continued woman hunt.

During the early morning hours of the next day, the North Shore of Long Island was not only swarmed with cops as two bodies identified as Maddy St. Hilaire and Deslyn Soprano lay on the beach. It was believed they had washed ashore. Their bodies seemed brutally mutilated and concussion laded.

According to detective Jamie Johnson:

"It looked like someone had not only used them as punching bags but according to their torn attire had viciously raped and strangled them."

Police helicopters littered the sky and coast guard boats swarmed the seas from the coast of Long Island to Connecticut – catching nothing in their nets.

It was now very apparent this investigation had turned into an escalated dilemma. Detectives Hobbs and Johnson embarked on the scene and tarried way after sunset. It was at dusk when they received a call: It was from the medical examiner who seemed to have worked overtime. The autopsy conducted on both girls revealed stunning perceptions.

"Whoever did this apparently know how to punch adeptly. As their trajectory was consistent with left jabs, right jabs, upper-cut and flush. The concussions seemed as if they were administered by a man with huge fists. We'll be working overnight to provide full discovery."

This seemed like an unusual cliff-hanging autopsy. Meanwhile, Detective Johnson spoke with a reporter and dropped this message:

"We need to act sooner than later. Any one of these girls could have been your sister or mine."

While the search for this mysterious predator continued, and law enforcement honed in on Long Island, the FBI went gleaning through other nearby cities. A tip led them to White Plains.

Every known Boxing Ring was visited and searched for any possible forensic or DNA linking to these teens, along with any evidence to verify if the predator had been in the system. After three days of searching, they came up with an empty net.

However, on day five of their expedition post the two girl's bodies washing up on Long Islands' North Shore, the FBI raided a Chop Shop in White Plains, New York. There were no clues a midnight blue SUV nor a mint green Land Rover had passed through that automobile butchery.

Even so, the Feds walked away loaded with three employees of that establishment in handcuffs, computers, cell phones and loads of cash. Backdropped with a chained door as well as a parking lot. They loaded them into vans and departed.

Three arrests nonetheless but this did not spin well in the media. Why were they arresting Chop Shop pundits while this predator was still at large? Sparking a rift between the Feds and the two Lead detectives. As to whose case it was, and the linkage of arrests which only had to do with the case. The credits became a toss-up between these two entities.

"At least, if the Feds were going to make those kinds of *off the beaten path's arrests,* they should securely keep them under wraps so as not to aggravate the lead detectives on the case.

"Anyway, Trump was never indicted but multiple offenders inside his clique were."

Stated one legal expert in the Feds defense.

"They know how to function lawfully."

Reasoned the Teen Advocate from the Williamsburg crime scene.

Knowingly, botched arrests have not only plagued the NYPD but stigmatized and infested it. For example, the choking death of Eric Garner in Staten Island and multiple most recent mishaps. Thus, certainly casting a shadow on crimefighting globally as well as sprinkling salt inside the wound as far as NYC was concerned.

Even though police had an agenda to get this predator off the streets. Many civilians were very reluctant in providing any assistance which could help them in their investigations. Except for the victim's parents, well-wishers and an eclectic group upholding the right arm of justice.

7

While the Westchester County gas station attendant swore on the Bible it was a possible transvestite attired Cop she saw walked inside the station. Placed, a one-hundred-dollar bill on the counter and said: "fill up!" walked back to the pump-side, filled it up with gas and drove away after a brawl broke out inside of the SUV.

While in a statement-collecting-mode. Hobbs and Johnson received the remainder of the autopsy report for the two murdered teen-girls Maddy St. Hilaire and Deslyn Soprano. Now conclusively, the report upped the story.

They refocused on the gas station attendant's account. However, that's all she wrote. all the information that the attendant captured in her confused state of mind before that assailant bounced, hitting the streets of Westchester.

Consequently, many pondered inside the media: If the predator was a male or most likely a female NYC cop who showed up at that Westchester gas station, she has accomplices rendering her bidding - working as a team or enterprise. Indicating law enforcement was missing multiple clues along the way.

Even though their talking point was:

"Catch this predator before he or she strikes again."

There was no image profile of this predator still at large. Instead, posted signs read: The predator was last seen posing as a male and now they are saying a female NYPD officer.

Although this was a step in the right direction it had dire consequences referencing a female cop. This idea selectively confused the heck out of female officers trying to do their jobs unshielded by a male partner.

Plus, with that alleged female persona acting like a cop and published in the media. An uncalculated move; any smart perpetrator will be otherwise prompted to change their propriety to prey on others undetected or from a standpoint of authority.

Meanwhile, in the mid-afternoon on that same day, yet another teen, the fourth, was abducted outside a recreation park. This time in Rochester, New York, and further north. This escalation left the two lead detectives scratching their heads.

One thing was clear to the lead detectives: Whoever was carrying out these abductions was flying low under the radar. With only that tidbit information to this point. They felt they were aggressively looking for a needle in a haystack.

"We have to go and talk to people. We can't expect them to come to us. We have to focus on being proactive. Them giving us a hand could be farfetched."
Said Johnson during a Cable TV interview.

"Parents are scared. Teens are humiliated. Sometimes it might be a stretch reaching out to us but we're here for you. We are here for your community. Please if you see something, say something and we promise you we'll do the rest."
Said Hobbs as if he were running for the *Mayorship*. Inside local barbershops and salons, the strategy of cops now needing the help of their communities was widely discussed. Although the commune was bleeding from the pain inflicted by this predator, many not trusting the cops were prepared to wear a band-aid on this new wound even it hurts them. Yep. That Eric Gardener's innocent killing like a thorn in their side still pricked them every time the cops said:

"We need your help."
It was by now a given: Law enforcement needed the public on board to aid their investigation. As sophisticated as their weaponry and intel, they had to solicit the help of civilians – boots on the ground.

Many civilians felt the chasm between them and law enforcement for way too long had been a one-way street. Removing that street sign would no doubt be a start toward ending the chaotic infrastructure between the police and civilians.

9

H ours later, that autopsy expanded report surprisingly revealed: Sperm was found in the genital area of both girls. According to the tests, the substance differed associated with both teens. Possibly transferred from two different men.

Focused on the written report, Hobbs looked across at Johnson, puzzled.

"Now the thought of a criminal serial enterprise looms large. There's pluralism."

He echoes.

Corroborating their findings, many pondered: If the predator was a female who had the audacity to disguise as an NYC cop, and who showed up at that Westchester County gas station. Was there a possible impersonator on their hands? Or were there copycats. They queried. She must have accomplices rendering her bidding - working as a team or enterprise insisted detective Johnson. Signifying law enforcement was missing some clues along the way and not closer to an arrest.

Even though one of their talking points was:

Catch this predator before he or she strikes again. They lacked the competence to wheel her in. Playing catch up distantly, unfortunately, was in their DNA. By now acquired no image profile of this predator still at large. Instead, posted signs read: The predator was last seen posing as a female NYPD officer. Yet, there was concrete evidence regarding sexual origin or gender.

"They were still malnourished evidentially."

Said the Teen Advocate, wannabe attorney from Williamsburg to an interviewer.

"Anybody could acquire a cop's uniform if they decided to play a bad actor."

Said, Detective Jonathan Hobbs without genuinely weighing the shortcomings of that statement. How? Although this sounded like it had validity it had dire consequences. This idea confused the heck out of female officers trying to do their jobs properly. Plus, with that alleged persona *acting like a cop* and published in the media resembled an uncalculated move. Why? Any smart perpetrator would be otherwise prompted to change their propriety to prey on their victim undetected.

Meanwhile, in the mid-afternoon on that same day, yet another teen was abducted outside a recreation park. Now the fourth abduction so far. This time in Rochester, New York, further north.

This escalation left the lead detectives scratching their heads. Evident there were so many questions yet very few answers.

10

While law enforcement expanded their hunt in upstate New York for the predator, news broke: The Gas Station attendant from that Westchester County gas station was now missing apparently abducted on her way home. Later that evening, the lone onlooker came forward, stating the attendant was waiting at the bus stop when the incident went down. Also vouching the hit was carried out by a Caucasian looking woman wearing an afro hairstyle as was described in the earlier abduction in White Plains.

Once again, it was reported: This abduction now the fifth like the others happened fast and furious. The onlooker was unable to recall much else, except it all, went down swiftly.

Westchester County police jointly with Hobbs and Johnson were busily putting the pieces together while conferring with other NYC agencies as well as the FBI. By sunrise, law enforcement had encamped at a vacant parking lot where the gas station attendant's body was discovered, brutally mutilated, raped and deep concussions to the face and head like what the other victims suffered.

Not since serial killer William Devon Howell, described as the drifter prowled in nearby Connecticut streets in 2003. Where he roamed the streets in his van dubbed his "murder mobile" did the Tri-State of New York, New Jersey and Connecticut encounter such brutal murderous seriality.

By then, not much-aided law enforcement in bringing down this predator. Howell back in 2003 had abducted, assaulted and murdered seven people who he buried in his garden behind a strip mall as a memorial.

Now, although a strong police presence remained in upstate New York. In less than five hours after the body of the gas station attendant was discovered, the body of the third victim from that Brooklyn Mall was discovered in a dense field in Westchester, New York. According to detective Jonathan Hobbs when he heard the news:

"Now it seems like that predator is acting as a killer on steroids, and must be immediately stopped."

11

L ater that evening. Responding to a tip out of Bethpage, Long Island. Detectives Hobbs and Johnson pulled up outside a house perched in a cul-de-sac with a mint-green Land Rover parked in its descendent driveway.

The home was partially lit and sunset was already history. Hobbs knocked first, then kicked the door in and entered in takedown style. Johnson provided cover. As Hobbs entered the house, a backup SWAT team encamped in front of the house.

Going through the side door and trying to get away, a slim and slender elderly man was trapped and commanded to drop his weapon. He retaliated at first but then expediently obliged. He was handcuffed and his Maranda rights read to him by detective Jamie Johnson.

Johnson shoved him inside on the rear seat of their Sedan. Moments later, the mint-green Land Rover was towed away from the driveway.

About an hour later, at the police station, Hobbs administered very strong interrogation tactics on the man who we now learned was Antonio Calderon, a man of Italian heritage and an ex-police officer with the NYPD. However, he checked out clean without any criminal past.

It seemed Calderon embellished having his rights read to him at his arrest as he thereafter remained tight-lipped as if he very much intended on pleading the fifth.

The Land Rover was thoroughly swept and hair particles of that third victim abducted from the Brooklyn Mall were lifted. Additionally, semen found thus far on and inside the bodies of three of four deceased victims matched Calderon's DNA.

Detectives Hobbs and Johnson felt certain based on evidence they had found one of their men, except Calderon refused to fess-up. According to the detectives he elected to remain tongue-tied.

If it wasn't for the semen found on the other girl's body which proved different from Calderon's the detectives might have cooled their heels upon his arrest.

12

For days on end, the news reverberated and spun in multiple rhetorical theoretical directions. "One down! They caved! They can run but they can't hide!" was the word on the streets. In the meantime, candlelight vigils in multiple communities, including Westchester County multiplied as mourners celebrated their dead. Counter-terrorism taskforce, as well as law enforcement entities, camped out at related sites for precautionary measures.

Early the following morning, tragedy struck once again. This time in Mt. Vernon, New York, where two teen girls were abducted in broad daylight outside Mt. Vernon High School. Victims now tolling seven.

It was later discovered: School surveillance camera harnessed on the school and which was supposed to be operable wasn't. Same scenario to the occurrence at that Williamsburg McDonalds.

Back on the hunt were detectives Hobbs and Johnson. They speedily embarked on Mt. Vernon looking for much-needed answers. All they got was suppositions and maybes. Some people claimed they saw the vehicle speeding through their neighborhood and like greased lightning it disappeared.

As Hobbs previously predicted:

"This predator is not a lone wolf going after our sheep. There's a team, a clique, an enterprise, and we've got to ax them. This may be a team effort but not bigger than us. We're the finest. The NYPD. We have standards to uphold – the highest."

In hindsight, it finally dawned on Hobbs that Calderon was too frail and slender, plus as an elderly man, he could not possibly land those alleged punches afflicted on those victims. Plus, he was small fisted, to say the least. Hobbs' awakening to this fact came after an additional autopsy report claimed one of the victims suffered a broken collar bone from a possible laden punch in the neck region.

Meanwhile, Johnson was still whispering in Hobbs's ear what should be done to Antonio Calderon for preying on these young girls. It was a chemically harsh punishment. She even entertained the idea of firstly, dusting off her karate skills on the elderly Calderon. Seemingly, he was elated preying on these young girls. She even claimed he was a centerfold torn out of Jeffrey Epstein's playbook.

13

At this stage of the investigation. An inquiry that began a little over two weeks ago in Williamsburg. Five teen girls were already abducted and murdered with their remains recovered. With two other teens unaccounted for. One perpetrator, Antonio Calderon was arrested and charged. Plus, three Chop Shop employees in White Plains, although not charged with any of these abductions or murders but got caught up in a sweep operation pursued by the FBI, were already behind bars.

In the interim, it was clear to law enforcement, whoever was currently orchestrating these hits on young teen girls was still at large and must cease and desist.

Many calls flowed into the department's switchboard geared to bring down the predator but to no avail. Multiple baiting scenarios spun out of control in the media and just about everywhere people congregated. Now, like a complicated upside-down jig-saw puzzle, all the pieces problematically didn't fit. Why? The probabilities regarding the true identity of the predator were still oblivious.

Even law enforcement, although not admittedly felt the uncanniness of the crime they were investigating. Some cops during their coffee breaks envisioned the investigation as a reincarnated Sherlock Holmes experience.

Additionally, Calderon's protectiveness to remain tight-lipped was distressing the detectives. There were no cell phone records to track his paths; as no phone was recovered upon his arrest.

Finally, synchronically a tip dropped. The lead detectives sensed they had collaboratively hit a home run.

At the latest abduction, it was reported: A police camera located on Main Street captured a profile of the villain adorned wearing a blonde wig while attempting that last getaway. This image was speedily transmitted to detectives Hobbs and Johnson at police headquarters and expediently distributed to every law enforcement agency in NYC.

It was almost dark and they wanted to take advantage of whatever daylight remained. Plus, a slight chance of snow was forecasted, and the weatherman jinxing mother nature; the area got blanketed. So, the night passed without another strike by the predator.

14

Early next morning before the crack of dawn, and snowplows still active, cops, like flies on molasses swarmed the streets of Westchester County looking for the predator. The name headlined their thinking - **Louise Dipson** an ex-NYPD officer.

Her profile reportedly had matched the description of the predator, connected in pulling off the abductees, rapes, and murders of those innocent teen girls. Detectives Hobbs and Johnson were confident; they now had something tangible to latch onto – a suspect. Most of all they were confident this was their woman and were resolute in stopping her before she struck again. They became heavy-footed.

Paradoxically, Hobbs sensed he was served a half-baked-cake. Realizing the gooeyness, he demanded the entire profile on Dipson. It seemed as if someone or a clique at the 71st Precinct in Brooklyn located at New York Avenue and Empire Blvd had suppressed most of Dipson's information.   Hobbs' detective partner Jamie Johnson read in and questioned:

"Why is this a drip, drip? What the hell are they hiding?"

"This seems like a total cover-up."

Responded Jonathan Hobbs.

It now hurried up and wait.

Hobbs got on his cell phone, reached out to their captain demanding Louise Dipson's entire profile. The stalled process was overturned when the captain intervened and later texted Hobbs but it was still drip, drip.

Louise Dipson worked at the NYPD in Crown Heights...
Yet, her connections were missing. Clearly, her profile was on lockdown. Hobbs and Johnson once again

demanded her entire profile and nothing less. Who she knew, who knew her, everything?

The Governor of New York was alerted and pressured the NYPD into coughing up Dipson's entire Bio. Challenged, the team of Connivers at that precinct though hesitantly, complied with the Governor's escalated demand.

15

L ouise Dipson's profile was rapidly unraveling in the media and elsewhere. More so than the Robert Mueller Report. *Louise Dipson was born to devout Catholic parents. They resided in Crown Heights, New York. A community mostly inhabited by orthodox Jews. Louise attended high school during those days of the Crown*

Height riots. It was during the tenure when NYC elected the first black mayor – Mr. Dinkins.

When Dinkin's term was at a low ebb, and the prosecutor from the Southern District Court of New York – Giuliani decided to challenge Dinkins for the mayorship and won. Louise Dipson joined the NYPD.

Her days prior to high school proved one to be reckoned with. She very seldom associated with the girls in her class and categorized them as weak. If you wanted to find her, look for where the boys hung out and there she was. Playing everything from 3-card-Monty and other trick games.

Louise played all the sports. You name the game and she enlisted. On evenings after school, she frequented the boxing rings in Brooklyn. Although under-aged to enter most of those facilities, she adopted the art of talking her way in, over, around, and out of situations. The guys loved hanging out with Louise and nicknamed her "The Dip."

One evening a brawl broke out after a boxing event. It was between two of the guys with whom she frequently hung out. She did not only referee the fight but took down both of the guys in whose hands she could easily crumble like an unleavened pretzel.

The boys thereafter set her apart as the girl no to mess with, and whichever boy group she affiliated with, they became fisted as steel.

Dipson learned how to throw a punch and it landed with a thud. When she frequented the club, other women envied her. It was said: "Louise could dance her A off and men flocked to her like a magnet"

The news descrambled and listeners and viewers became glued to their gadgets.

16

L ouise Dipson never got married. Many wondered Why? Some claimed, whoever the man was to become hitched with Louise had it coming as he would definitely have a tussle on his hands with: revenge deep-seated in her psyche.

Her mother Ellen Dipson passed on when Louise was only 19 years of age, the result of a motorist mauling a pedestrian in Crown Heights.

Weeks later, the driver, a Jamaican immigrant was arrested in conjunction with the accident. He not only posted a strong defense but onlookers testified her mother crossed the street at Utica Avenue and Eastern Parkway while the traffic light was still green. The driver claimed it was a foggy night and he was later acquitted. This didn't sit too well with Dipson even though her mother suffered from the disease Alzheimer's.

Louise remained on edge and was of the opinion the light was yellow and turning red instead of green and turning yellow as stated. That motorist, it was alleged, hauled her mother under his *illegal taxi's* chassis for many blocks.

"It was just before sunset on a Friday. He should have known that he was driving through a predominantly Jewish neighborhood where its residents were always rushing to complete their tasks just before sundown on Fridays, pursuant to welcoming in the Sabbath. The bell had already chimed in Crown Heights and he should have heard it…dah?"

She lamented.

Louise, along with her friends, mostly Jewish, organized and picketed against the upcoming West Indian Day parade on Eastern Parkway that year. She was successful in getting the attention of not only the predominantly Jewish community but the media as well. Protest related signs were stapled on just about every light pole in Brooklyn.

However, the revenue generated from this event which attracted millions of tourists to NYC on Labor Day weekend far outweighed any plans to derail the Labor Day festivities. Plus, the City Council had their hands deep inside the till.

17

L ater that fall, Louise Dipson attended the Police Academy and became an NYPD officer. It wasn't long before she walked the beat in Crown Heights, with her chest stuck out and her gun visibly protruding from its holster. Always ready to cite violators of the law - she telegraphed.

Dipson, speedily earned her stripes with the NYPD and within only a few short years, she was tapped to head up a team of officers, instrumental in bringing down a prostitution ring on Buffalo Avenue and East New York Avenue. About half a mile north of Crown Heights. For this clean sweep operation, she earned numerous accolades as the rookie cop who shook that prostitution ring loose.

Her love interest at the department was Captain Jerome Meeks, who endowed her with pleasantries. Gossiped at the department: "Captain Meeks is single so why don't they tie the knot?"

Conversely, this truism: *Familiarity breeds contempt* borne out. It wasn't long before Louise Dipson was sleeping with some of those pimps, she chased off the block at Buffalo Avenue. They subsequently relocated to mid-town Manhattan and Dipson became Miss NYPD uniformed in the daytime and Pimp Daddy's pet and his play bunny at nights.

Pimp Daddy, the flamboyant and classy dresser. Seen most times in a trench coat and a cigar in his mouth. One of the few men empowered to curb Louise. Instinctively, he kept her under heavy manners.

The NYPD busted Louise one night as they supplanted a deep undercover unit in that newly formed Manhattan prostitution ring, the locale where she patronized. It was later revealed, the undercover officer offered to pay Louise much more than the going rate.

However, Jerome Meeks, oblivious to Louise Dipson shared a triangular relationship with Nicole Best, a higher-up at Internal Affairs. A conflict of interest? He clearly saw his future with Nicole Best who was known for throwing her weight around and frequented major governmental circles extended as far as Washington, DC.

Louise Dipson suddenly felt his cold shoulder. It took only a month for Internal affairs to state their findings and Louise was terminated without pay.

Meanwhile, her stomach grew. Most of her peeps encouraged her to abort the fetus. Louise refused; bent on her staunch Catholic upbringings.

Her daughter Cherae Louise Dipson was born almost seven months later. Now still without adequate employment and a young one to take care of. Louise became penniless and resorted to welfare support. Like a sliding iceberg, she went downhill. Louise Dipson eventually collected and sold soda and beer cans.

Bouncing back, she took a job at a local supermarket bagging grocery. To her dismay, many of those violators she cited while being strapped.

Subsequently, she worked her way up the ladder with that Supermarket giant and by the time Cherae was ready to attend high school she positioned herself as the store manager.

18

Louise Dipson, ardently cemented deep in the annals of New York law enforcement taught her daughter whatever street smarts she deemed relevant. So much that her Cherae swaggered, cherishing being endowed with that upper hand.

"Although I've never done everything my mother wanted. I'm very mindful of all that she taught me."

Those words echoed from her mother and through the fertile mind of young Cherae.

The young Dipson was a straight "A" student at Crown Heights High and seemed destined to steer her way through law school at John Jay College, upon which, she very early sat her sights as a supreme litigator. As a leader in all sports as well as the Associated Student Body she excelled.

During the Parkland School shootings in Florida a few years ago, Cherae encapsulated the tragedy as:

"That will never happen in NYC. Not in my school!"

Cherae bonded with a handful of students including Nikia Chavez. On one hot summer's day in July a year later, Cherae did not return from school. A search went out for days throughout the five Boroughs for the missing model student from Crown Heights High. There was not a trace. Zilch. Nada. Zip. Zero! She disappeared without a trace.

New York law enforcement hit the streets vehemently. After a week of futility, a partially decomposed girl's body was found deep in a Westchester County Park Woodlands aided by vultures.

After an autopsy, it revealed the girl's body which was brutally mutilated, with multiple stabbed wounds and evidence of rape was Cherae Dipson's. It seemed like that was water under the bridge.

However, two years later, on what would have been Cherae's eighteenth birthday, the two teens Deslyn Soprano and Maddy St. Hilaire were abducted from the parking lot of that McDonald's fast-food restaurant in another close-knit community - Williamsburg, New York.

19

With all that backstory in play. The lead detectives in the investigation of the alleged predator, Hobbs and Johnson not only knew who they were looking for but influenced a large segment of the New York populous to call on the Governor to step up police street patrol statewide.

The cover on Louise Dipson's Facebook page with her daughter backdropped read: *An eye for an eye. A tooth for a tooth.*

Several weeks after Louise Dipson began her menacing rampage on young teen girls the most intense search for her so far was carried out.

Paradoxically, it was recorded as one of the slowest nights of citations since the department birthed on New Year's Day 1898.

Just after 9:00 AM the following morning, instead of dragging this predator inside their net, tragedy once again struck. This time outside a train station at Dyre Ave close to the border of Bronx and Mt. Vernon. The final stop on the # 5 Train. All passengers on this train had already disembarked including Carla DeFreitas and Camille Glasgow, two girls in their mid-teens who mostly grouped together and known as C.C.

Backpack laden, they rushed through the turnstiles to catch the waiting bus which now became mobile leaving smoke in their faces. The two girls, frustrated with the total let down. Dropped their guard somewhat.

Louise Dipson saw them unhinged and adeptly pounced into their space. By the time onlookers zeroed in on the unfolding scene - Dipson had already shoved the two girls inside her abduct-mobile – midnight blue SUV and drove away speedily.

Later, one of those onlookers, who preferred to remain anonymous claimed:

"The entire episode transpired so darn fast. By the time I realized what was happening, the SUV with a hard to read license tag turned the corner north on Dyre Avenue and sped out of sight towards the Westchester County border. At this point, I yelled out 'Help! Somebody, please help!' No one dared.

A motorist driving an illegal taxi cab. I believe he did hear my scream for help. Instead of chasing behind the perpetrator, he headed in the opposite direction. Reading his lips, he seemed to be saying:

"You must be mad! I and I no get in involved in stuff like that. A cockroach doesn't have any business in cock foul party."

It was then I called 911 on my iPhone. The police took forever to arrive. They were not even able to play catchup in pursuant of that SUV which by then had an enormous head-start on its getaway route.

Detective Hobbs and Johnson on the scene documented her statement and corroborated it with Louise Dipson's profile.

20

As was done before: after Dipson first struck in Williamsburg, road-blocks were once again set up. The Mt. Vernon police collaborated in the search for those missing girls.

This time mostly along exit off and on-ramps. Traffic on the Major Deacon Expressway crawled heading north towards the Canadian border. Even though heading north for Dipson would put her at risk unless she exited before crossing the Canadian border. There her vehicle would no doubt get searched and swept by Canadian border patrols. Mounted police were poise and armed just in case Dipson dared cross over into Canadian territory. The news of this NYC based serial abductor had already saturated the CBC airwaves in Buffalo, New York and across the border.

Contrariwise, heading south could also be a risky proposition to make as the Bronx River Parkway, the George Washington Bridge heading into New Jersey and the Henry Hudson Parkway heading into Manhattan's westside, were baited traps in waiting for this getaway SUV.

Law Enforcement was now getting into Dipson's psyche. As she cleverly navigated those side streets in upper-New York. They were clever at determining how one of their own would think in all those given circumstances. Even so, Louise Dipson countered.

Except once again she enticed them on a wild goose chase. They looked for her on the major streets. In the meantime, she rolled along the side streets. Dipson was never found so they once again found themselves sucking their thumbs.

How they wished someone would say:

"I saw something. A vehicle looking like Dipson's. Anything."

It was not a case wherein she was stationary. But she was clever enough to travel underneath their radar. Always one step ahead of any of their blueprints to catch her. Anything for them to go on. Victims numbers 8 and 9 abductees had already gotten stuck in her spider web and became deeply entangled. Now she was on a quest for more victims and desperately had to be stopped before she struck again.

Multiple scenarios bombarded the minds of Hobbs and Johnson. The chess game was on and Dipson focused on how to strategically move all her King-men every time they blinked. She knew as long as they didn't stop her, she held the upper hand. Already there were multiple questions with still limited answers. Some New Yorkers entertained: "The Internal Affairs should have gone easy on Dipson when she prostituted. Plus, getting pregnant was not only her right but it was her body and not someone else's."

No matter what analogy they used to describe her cop-turned-teen-predator-persona. She was putting them to the test and not only using up their mental faculties and resources for her own selfish benefit but predating on those innocent girls. Teens who had nothing to do with the death of her daughter, Cherae.

21

For days it seemed as if the entire investigation was put on deep freeze. Inside the department, the lead detectives Hobbs and Johnson gave the impression as if their hands were completely tied behind their backs. While displaying a total façade.

They were now information-laden and ultimately-result-empty.

Even so, news continued circulating and spun out of control in the media. *The predator could be lurking in your neighborhood.* Freedom of Press could be an investigative monster at times. They continually kept the public on high alert. While some complained law enforcement wasn't doing enough to solve these crimes and bringing the predator to justice. The press stayed constant.

It was clear Dipson was not the average wannabe criminal. She was adept, a notch above the rest. According to her profile archived by NYPD, she was street smart, law enforcement savvy, and physically fit. Additionally, she knew how to get in and out of any situation and eventually trap her pursuers while doing so. In short, going after this predator they realized they had their hands full.

On the other hand, most believed with all this beefed-up presence put in place by the Governor of New York, it could be just a matter of time before she plunged inside their baited net. However, in order to do so, these two detectives realized they had to bring their "A" game. They kept sorting bait. The water was warm but their bait wasn't suitable for catching that fish.

Tick! Tick! The clock was ticking fast and young teen girls were more scared of the outdoors even when accompanied by an adult. Additionally, not only the police but parents and teachers were also on edge. They wanted the predator captured before she struck again. Not tomorrow, next week, next month or next year but now. One more parent in peril over the disappearance of their teen girl was more than NYC could handle.

While these talking points festered. News broke that two park rangers saw a flock of vultures frequenting the woodlands of Westchester County. They followed their lead and subsequently discovered two bodies deep in the Westchester County woodlands. A location close to where the body of Cherae Dipson was found more than two years ago.

Police helicopters were dispatched and soon circled overhead as these two brutally mutilated bodies of the last teens abducted at Dyre Avenue in the Bronx were airlifted in body-bags and out of that bereaved commune.

22

With fingers continually pointing at Louise Dipson the predator. Law enforcement once again had it right. The bodies of those two teen girls bore the same resemblance of those previously abducted in the last two months and linked to Louise Dipson. Now bringing the sting of murders to nine.

Neighbors in that Westchester community, and residing close to the woodlands were particularly questioned. Yet, no one claimed they saw anything or encountered anyone driving a midnight blue SUV by day or night.

The lead detectives, Hobbs and Johnson were now more frantic than ever. Nothing they've done so far led them to catch this predator who kept leaving dead bodies behind a sign she was still active.

It became apparent detectives were looking for a needle in a haystack or what some classified a wild goose chase.

Consequently, they revisited Calderon in prison. Hobbs, before coming up with the idea to make this visit, decided he was going to once again press Calderon for answers. Hoping he would drop some bread crumbs. Johnson approved. Hobbs entertained the idea that if Calderon was somehow promised a light sentence, he might consider flipping. Thus, providing answers to assist in capturing Dipson.

They were cognizant of this one fact: In the past perpetrators indicted by the Southern District of New York court were apt to become rats in order to reduce their sentence. Aiding prosecutors to their ultimate target.

Hobbs, on this particular visit, was even willing to offer Calderon full immunity in order for him to fully cooperate as per the prosecutors. Yet, Calderon would not buy-in. He preferred keeping his cards close to his chest.

Calderon's defense liked what the detectives were offering his client. They felt this would eventually let him off the hook. To all this, he said:

"I cannot be a RAT. I would rather suffer the consequences. I'm an old man and could die soon, prison or no prison. So, with that said, I prefer to let sleeping dogs lie. It's water under the bridge as far as I can see it."

This frustrated the two detectives. Hobbs reached for his gun, stuck it inside Antonio Calderon's mouth as Calderon was in a "Ha hah. I'm not going to rattle on anyone. Put that in your pipe and smoke it – mode."

Hobbs released the gun's safety threatening to waste Calderon.

"Who else was complicit in this serial spree, preying on young teens?"

Asked Hobbs.

Calderon gasped, he choked and stood up with bent knees. Hobbs stood up giving himself necessary leverage to accommodate a direct deepthroated pallet removal.

"Sam…Saamy!"

Uncomfortably asked Calderon.

"Sammy who?"

Asked the two detectives in a touché mode.

"Sammy Grant!"

Belched Calderon.

At this stage, the Lieutenant walked in and Hobbs released his draw. Now with a name to go on. Johnson winked at Hobbs; knowing they had a principal.

They departed embolden. However, the department stonewalled with regard to the information on Sammy Grant's whereabouts.

23

L ater that day. The FBI raided the home of Louise Dipson in Crown Heights. She was not there. However, they hauled away computers, boxes of documents and picture portraits.

The following morning Louise Dipson struck yet again in an unrelated locale. This time outside a grocery store in the South Bronx. In broad daylight, yet another teen girl was abducted.

An astute onlooker ventured in pursuit. However, he encountered problems as he tried starting up his pickup truck. When he finally got it started. An eighteen-wheeler had double-parked moments before and blocking his exit. The motorist blew his vehicle's horn constantly to no avail.

In the meantime, he dialed 911 on his iPhone. By the time the driver of the eighteen-wheeler returned to set him free from that parking spot, detective Hobbs and Johnson previously stationed at the Dyre Avenue subway station, bore down onto the scene in their unmarked sedan.

Instantly, additional Police vehicles swarmed the street like bees on a beehive. The now relieved motorist points them north. They pursued hastily northbound as a convoy - raced.

For miles, they traveled like Alice in Wonderland. Suddenly as if miraculously, they caught up with that midnight blue mud layered SUV pulling out of a gas station.

Now multiple car lengths ahead it left them in the dust. The number of police vehicles in tow increased. Johnson in the passenger seat of their sedan logged in its temporary license tags only to find the search came back - invalid.

Already on high alert, instantaneous roadblocks created a detour instead of a flytrap. As if sensing their directives, the motorist in the SUV still oblivious to the pursuing lead detectives sensed their angle and orchestrated an individual diversion. The effects of this detour were only temporary.

The SUV ramped onto a two-lane highway leading away from the City's limits and through the woodlands. Police vehicle sirens crescendo as cops blazed ahead in pursuit. Overhead helicopters join the search. The two lead detectives in the front car of this convoy were now bearing down on this runaway SUV with guns drawn.

While thick shrubbery barred the Ariel vision. Unpredictably, a slow-moving deer crossed the street in front of the lead sedan.   The cruiser slammed into the animal turned a 90-degree angle in the road. Meanwhile, this tailing vehicle slammed into its rear fender and those on each other's tail into their lead.

Helicopter police notified of multiple-car pile-up tried landing but aborted the mission due to insufficient wingspan accommodation and dense fog. With the chase curtailed in a vehicular pileup, officers assess the damage and licked their wounds. As Hobbs regained his presence of mind he radioed in for assistance.

It was relayed back via text:

The name Sammy Grant loomed largely. Sammy's semen sample was found in and on all the girls who were abducted and murdered since Louise Dipson began to prowl.

Law enforcement had been staking out in front of Sammy's house in Crown Heights, Brooklyn using Crown Heights Security Patrol vehicles. Ironically, it seemed his house had no dwellers as delivered mail was hanging out of his mailbox.

It now became a sudden toss-up for Hobbs and Johnson. Continue going after Louise Dipson or concentrate on the bird in hand, Sammy Grant? The pursuit of Dipson ran cold while news of Sammy Grant simmered. Soon police helicopters circling overhead retreated.

The NYPD ended up slowing their roll in pursuit of Louise Dipson minutes later. She had already eluded them and vanished.

With the search now impaired as Dipson's getaway had occurred. Hobbs and Johnson followed their tip which led them to Crown Heights, Brooklyn on that Friday evening. The close-knit Jewish neighborhood with its own CHSP units, Ambulance fleet, and multiple street cameras. It was a planned off night for the CHSP.

Going undercover in an unmarked vehicle served the detectives well as to not disturb the community on the eve of their sabbath. Every door for business now closed except for the neighborhood Cleaners, barricades moved in place along Eastern Parkway and Kingston Avenue.

Sammy Grant's house nestled among one of these establishments. It became a growing concern for the commune as the FBI had recently raided Louise Dipson's house in that same neighborhood, a few days prior.

As the detectives pulled up. Grant was on his way out. "How convenient!"

Hobbs whispered to Johnson. They made the calculated arrest and read him his Maranda Rights. Multiple unmarked police vehicles converged on Kingston Avenue and Eastern Parkway as Sammy was hauled away on the Sabbath's eve.

24

Before booking Sammy Grant on charges. The two lead detectives endeavored to get as much as they can out of him. He was more cooperative than Calderon. In that, he confessed he was complicit with Calderon in assaulting and raping those young girls. Additionally, he was tied to the string of abductions with Louise Dipson. It was becoming obvious Grant was leaning towards becoming an informant even without his legal counsel present.

While the news of Sammy Grant's arrest percolated in the media. Pimp Daddy's name became a high priority on the lead detective's list. Once the New York pimp's name dropped, they became busily connecting the dots.

On the other hand, Grant told the authorities he joined the team due to Pimp Daddy's solicitation. Grant provided in his statement that he became involved with the girls in conjunction with Pimp Daddy and Antonio Calderon. Grant even stated he paid Pimp Daddy to sleep with these girls. When asked if he later shared the girls with Calderon. He stated:

"Calderon was a man of enormous wealth and paid his own way."

"Calderon was a business mogul in operation for most of his adult life."

Said Sammy Grant.

The can of worms was now ajar in this investigative process. In other words: Drip by drip the giant rock was being unseated. When questioned in regard to Dipson, Grant, however, remained tight-lipped.

"What was he hiding? Why was he trying to protect Dispson?"

The detectives queried during their lunch recess. When they returned and regrouped those questions were once again raised. Sammy Grant adeptly dogged the Dipson bullet.

"If Grant wanted immunity it was clear he had to come clean and give up all the necessary information relating to his crimes. Including any or all in complicit to Dipson.

Bolstered, Detective Johnson.

It was obvious, Dipson already spearheaded this operation and whatever it took to lead detectives to her before she struck again would be beneficial to the detectives in parceling their investigation. Yet, Grant in relation to Dipson sat on everything Louise Dipson. Hobbs and Johnson were now busily going through Pimp Daddy's profile after Grant floated his name.

At one point, Pimp Daddy was the wealthiest pimp in NYC. No wonder Calderon aligned himself with the Pimp. Not only that, he was the father of Cherae Dipson, Louise's daughter.

As a result of his involvement with Louise Dipson while she worked for the NYPD, Louise was terminated from the department after an internal affairs investigation possibly influenced by her boss Captain Jerome Meeks. Nevertheless, Pimp Daddy still had her back.

25

At daybreak, Hobbs and Johnson arrested Pimp Daddy in Westchester exiting a local bar. They tried to get whatever they could from Pimp Daddy in terms of a confession. He as in the case of Calderon remained tight-lipped. Their cover-up was growing more teeth.

The detectives felt certain if they could get Pimp Daddy to eventually come clean, they could possibly bring down Louise Dipson. Meanwhile, there was no information on the last girl who was abducted outside that Bronx Convenient Store. With Dipson still at large law enforcement remained on edge.

The attorneys representing Calderon in a Cable News interview claimed their client would be willing to clear his name. If given a chance to do so on TV. It was apparent, two of Calderon's associates were now indicted and incarcerated he could be in deep waters.

That was good news as people glued to the case wanted to hear from this elderly man who kept his mouth shut. Even so, they remained optimistic he would be willing to move the needle in their investigation.

On the other hand, as if suffering from Alzheimer's, by the time Calderon's defense brought him to the pond he wouldn't drink. Life imprisonment or not.

Causing TV anchors to wait in vain.

The prosecution felt as if Calderon, an adept gambler was taking them on a wild goose chase. One day he wanted to fess up. Then he chose not to say a word.

In a conversation between Hobbs and Johnson off the record Hobbs told Johnson:

"When it comes to Calderon's statement, we are going to have to get to Dipson even without his help. Too bad Sammy Grant wouldn't give us a window when it comes to Louise Dipson. What a freaking unadulterated cover-up!"

26

While the news of Sammy Grant and Pimp Daddy's arrest reached Louise Dipson. She had just completing masking herself and heading out to capture her next victim. Walking out of her hotel room she looked at her most recent victim twisting in pain and tied up with ropes to the bed frame. She was eventually stung with a change of heart.

Shaking her head, Louise Dipson closed the door to her hotel room and departed. Up the street and several blocks away she boarded that midnight blue SUV and departed. Purposed in her mind it was time to do it solo.

Louise was well known for exerting her independence. Even without Pimp Daddy in the picture. She felt she had this.

Immediately, she tapped into that vein and instead of calling the police and surrender she drove herself to the police station, parked the SUV on the parking lot, throw the keys on the passenger seat, locked the abduction-mobile, walked away and entered the Bronx Police Station.

Multiple police officers met her at the door in take-down style. Not that they were expecting her but they saw in their surveillance video when the SUV pulled up and made sure even their desk officers were fully armed for combat.

Dipson casually put her hands over her head at their command. They rushed in, frisked her and administered handcuffs. As the news spread. It surprised most law enforcement that Louise Dipson turned herself in. After running for weeks unleashed.

However, with her accomplices now behind bars. They felt she was subordinated and wearied.

According to Hobbs:

"Dipson had no choice but to give herself up to us. She's is tired of playing the cat and mouse game. Now she has been declawed…"

27

The news disseminated exponentially.

"Louise Dipson the predator gave herself up to law enforcement in the Bronx."

"The fast-food business is now operating full throttle." Expressed one Vegan enthusiast showing off a celery stick.

Parents, teens, churches, schools, as well as other teen-related institutions, were now all rendering PRAISE for what had transpired. She was finally off the streets. Now they were free to conduct business as usual.

On the other hand, some remained skeptical that Dipson might still be at large. They watched the news over and over again for comfort in the fact she had ceased and desist. Some even called the NYPD to ensure Dipson was securely behind bars.

The facts bore out. It was corroborated by the Governor's office: The Predator had cooled her heels. Now they were free to conduct business as usual.

It is said:

"With every new level, there's a new Devil."

That truism bore fruit as now law enforcement's new problem dangled as they focused on potential copy-cats. "What if others replicated her actions?" They whined. After coming to grips. They realized Louise Dipson was involved in a vendetta.

See, after Dipson's surrender to law enforcement, they realized she was partly acting out of revenge for her daughter Cherae's death. As was mentioned, the girl's body was recovered from the woodlands in Westchester County, raped, and brutally mutilated. Whoever conducted those brutal acts were still a mystery.

On the other hand, it was determined, if Sammy Grant would truly cooperate. Those charges against him could disintegrate. It seemed he was prepared to tease law enforcement with one foot in and one foot out.

That talking point simmered in the media as well as the legal arena for days. Now like a popcorn effect more evidence in the case popped up.

Now, DNA tests linked Sammy Grant to the rape of Cherae Dipson. It was determined: The semen specimen found at the crime scene of the young Dipson as well as multiple other sexual assault victims matched Sammy Grant's DNA.

So, even though Grant felt warm in the prosecutors' pocket. Those cold winds of two years ago had returned like a Northeaster to chill his butt.

On the other hand, Dipson was fighting with those tentacles of surrender. She refused from providing information leading to the whereabouts of her last victim. As she wavered through the night. In the wee hours of the morning, a hotel housekeeper at the Bronx Hotel discovered the victim Nikia Chavez tied to the bed frame of the hotel's bed frame.

28

As the Breaking News in this convoluted Dipson episodic spread. Pimp Daddy and Louise Dipson, now on bail, collectively filed a lawsuit against Sammy Grant for the unlawful death of their daughter Cherae Dipson.

The rumor became widespread; Pimp Daddy could have obliviously been the one responsible for bringing Sammy Grant on board this killing spree on the behest of Louise Dipson.

It was also widespread: Calderon and Grant both paid hefty sums for their involvement with those teen girls and regarded as pedophiles.

Once again Hobbs and Johnson went back to the drawing board and quizzed Calderon to see if he was ready to spill more beans. Anything about his collaboration with Grant at this point could set this investigation into overdrive they reckoned. However, Calderon once again remained mute.

On the other hand, Grant, when asked about his involvement in the rape and murder of Cherae Dipson, he resorted to pleading the fifth on that matter. Thus, leaving the prosecution stuck with a contaminated witness – himself.

As if miraculously, the lawsuit against Sammy Grant superseded the Louise Dipson and company trial in SDNY.

There erupted a keen sense of public sentiment for the suit brought against Sammy Grant by Louise Dipson and Pimp Daddy. Ironically, the defense team of Samuel Taliaferrow and Calista Cochran was retained and a court date set at SDNY.

Dipson and Pimp Daddy very much liked the odds delivered in the previous Brad versus Beverly Tyson –

Smith case in which Brad Smith was acquitted. To them, Taliaferrow was their hometown hero and Cochran their Big Apple heroine.

29

The first day of this lawsuit Louise Dipson and Pimp Daddy versus Sammy Grant captured the media's attention. Outside on the steps leading to inside the courthouse the lectern, littered with media microphones waited. Louise Dipson walked up to the microphones wearing GPS ankle bracelets. Claiming she could have been set up.

"By who?"

One reporter asked.

"You know who."

Replied Louise Dipson.

At this point, her layer Samuel Taliaferrow interceded: "This is a case in which we're seeking justice for the murder of the young teen Cherae Dipson. After two years, we are happy to be positioned to move this case forward."

That's all the news media got as they were left hanging for more. However, they took what they got and ran with it. She was mute when she turned herself into law enforcement. Plus, she has been quiet in public since. In this opportunity at the lectern that's all she wrote, and they expediently published it.

Spinning it every which way they could. Compounded with the talking point that the community of Crown Heights was torn. Jewish neighbors of the Dipsons joined in a community demonstration and pleaded for a conviction of Sammy Grant also from their neighborhood.

On the one hand, they nurtured a teen killer in Sammy Grant. Many now saw his residence as a sore eye in the Crown Heights community.

Sammy Grant had not only raped and murdered one of their teen idols but he was alleged to be complicit in the rape and death of nine other young teen girls.

30

Opening arguments swiftly began inside the courtroom at SDNY. The prosecution argued that Sammy Grant, a known murderer now sentenced for 20 years to be served in Attica, New York for the killing of Cherae Dipson. He previously hitched himself to the wagon of Pimp Daddy, Calderon and Louise Dipson enabling him to continue his killing spree. An event that stemmed from over two years ago with Cherae Dipson.

During the cross-examination of Pimp Daddy, it was revealed that Louise Dipson who retained the rights not to testify, was coerced into the seriality of young teen girls by defendant Sammy Grant.

On the other hand, it was brought to bear that Sammy Grant along with Calderon funded the operation. The prosecutors tried hard not to mix both cases involving Grant's criminality.

Even so, it was not an easy task as Grant's criminal activities were already baked into the cake. It had become obvious; Sammy Grant was adept at what he did. At the time he joined the Louise Dipson team and, in some ways, spearheaded her criminal operation.

Both Louise Dipson and Pimp daddy were not aware Grant was solely responsible for the killing of their daughter Cherae Dipson at the time he joined their squad.

Pimp Daddy was asked by the defense:

"If you had the chance to do it all over again what would be his strategy?"

To which he responded.

"I've never wanted to roll that way but with the promptings of Sammy Grant, and his skill set, it became apparent we could work together not knowing much of his criminal past. Wished I knew before he murdered our daughter."

31

Sammy Grant, on the other hand, claimed he had nothing to do with the death of Cherae Dipson. Even though Grant's DNA placed him fairly and squarely not only at the murder scene but as a sexual connect.

It was clear Sammy Grant anticipated he would get away with this two-year-old murder of the young Dipson which came back to haunt him. He, evidently flew under the radar for some time as law enforcement was unable to nab him as the brutal murderer in that murder case.

Sammy Grant, knowingly joined forces with Pimp Daddy, Calderon, and Louise Dipson.

" Sammy Grant enlisted himself as the catalyst."

Said Pimp Daddy.

"He was a prizefighter and very good in the ring. A man who can land a punch so hard his opponent would fall immediately to the ground."

Said a Sports Reporter who also claimed:

"As a fighter, Sammy Grant emulated the fighting tactics of the Heavy Weight Boxer – Mike Tyson."

It was also discovered, those victims who bore evidence of the brutality traced to those concussions were inflicted by someone with – Sammy Grant's sized hands.

Louise Dipson, sitting inside that courtroom broke down in tears as the pictures of the murder scene where Cherae's body was discovered, screen-slide and introduce again in this duplicitous murder saga. She made the sign of the cross on multiple occasions.

Pimp Daddy realized how deeply involved Louise Dipson was in the criminal enterprise, and a non-testifying witness, so he took the brunt of the beating from Grant's defense. They labeled Pimp Daddy not only as an accomplice in the murder of those teen girls but as a pimp he decided he would not get off the trail. So, he downscaled his operation. Instead, he decided to prey on young girls.

Pimp Daddy's distance from the new string of seriality for which he was indicted hung over his head like a thick cloud and even rained inside the courtroom as Louise Dipson teared up some more.

32

Meanwhile, Sammy Grant at one point, endeavoring to cast blame pointed fingers at both Pimp Daddy and Louise Dipson as the possible killers of their own daughter Cherae. Some claimed he had three fingers pointing back at him.

Additionally, Grant claimed during a conversation with Pimp Daddy the infamous NYC Pimp disclosed he liked young girls. Mainly around the ages of 14 – 17. There was no meat in that statement seeing it was just hearsay argued the prosecution. However, in this decade that talking point was relevant seeing one of the infamous young teen girl sexual offenders was recently incarcerated and subsequently committed suicide while incarcerated.

Also, Sammy Grant alluded to Pimp Daddy being intoxicated constantly. Therefore, he could have been an incest participant in his daughter's death.

That anecdote was ludicrous in the eyes of the jury as frowns were detected on some faces. Even so, Grant was willing to push the lid on this supposition. He further stated:

"When it comes down to sexual assault, he wouldn't put anything past Pimp Daddy due to his tenure as a notorious pimp."

Once again, all of this smelled like a smoking gun but without any fire.

The jury of 12 returned a guilty verdict in this lawsuit against Sammy Grant. However, it was discovered Sammy Grant was out of money. In other words, he looked good, smelled good but was physically flat broke. The only asset to his name was that brownstone home which he owned in Crown Heights according to sources handling his depleted finances.

Additionally, during his sentencing, he received 20 years in prison for the murder of Cherae Dipson. Her parents were awarded in the lawsuit his $750.000.00 Brownstone in Crown Heights. However, still, on the docket in SDNY the trial in which Grant was also indicted for participating in the killing of 9 other young teen girls in New York.

33

W hile jurors were being selected in the upcoming Louise Dipson the Predator, Pimp Daddy, Sammy Grant and Calderon versus the Government trial. Many legal scholars, as well as the media, very much anticipated the testimony of Nikia Gomez the lone survivor in this abduction spree. It was widespread among some of her peers. Nikia got what she deserved. Mainly because she hung out with the wrong crowd.

Previously, Nikia lived in Crown Heights, Brooklyn and attended CHH. Moving to the Bronx she underwent a complete makeover. Nikia not only changed her hairstyle bur added multiple nose rings and tattoos. Nothing about her resembled the Nikia of Crown Heights.

Living in the Bronx, she was known to have defied just about every curfew issued by her adopted parents. It was reported: Her parents were summoned to a Parent Teacher's meeting after a crack pipe was discovered inside her locker. To which Nikia claimed she didn't know how it got there.

Additionally, some of those same peers had reported her drug dilemma not only to other students but to teachers and the principals as well. In that school, Nikia was categorized as a basket case. However, she was the sole victim out of all alleged abductees conducted by Dipson still alive.

During Nikia's testimony, the prosecution armed themselves with as much evidence they possibly could. Their objective, even though Louise Dipson had lost her daughter Cherae Dipson, murdered by Sammy Grant, they not only wanted to see Louise Dipson rot in prison but possibly fry in the electric chair.

The media in the intervening time, did an entire spin on the trial, stating Dipson was guilty of all these crimes even before any witnesses were introduced in this trial.

Additionally, Nikia in her statement to detective Hobbs and Johnson, claimed she was raped once by Sammy Grant and that he threatened to do it again if she did not cooperate sexually. This was said to her a day before Louise Dipson turned herself in.

The forensic DNA evidence also linked Sammy Grant to Nikia. She claimed Grant carried out her abduction by throwing a bag over her head. Coincidentally, Nikia in a statement to the detectives said: She eluded innuendos made by Sammy Grant while she attended CHH as he frequented the neighborhood's post office across from the school. She broke down talking about guarding Cherae on the basketball court.

The prosecutor opined Nikia would administer the keypunch in the trial and was poised for the trial to get underway. While the New York toughest maximum-security prison waited with outstretched tentacles for the criminals involved in the serial enterprise.

34

The trial eventually began and after opening arguments the prosecution brought the infamous detectives Johnson followed by Hobbs to the stand.

Detective Johnson claimed she and her partner were first called to the McDonald's parking lot in

Williamsburg. It was in response to a 911 call regarding the abduction of two teen girls – Deslyn Soprano and Maddy St. Hiliare.

She stated upon arrival, the parking lot was practically filled with neighbors, friends, and the two sets of discombobulated parents.

"They never got into any trouble."

Claimed Deslyn Soprano's parents approaching before we could get out of our cruiser.

Meanwhile, the manager of that McDonalds, Angie Gomez headed in our direction all bent out of shape. We accommodated Gomez's statement in a separate huddle. She told us:

"The girls looked like they were about fourteen. They made their purchase and instead of eating in they opt to head outside." She gushed.

"Suddenly, as if by a flash of lightning a midnight-blue SUV pulled up, the girls were rushed inside on the rear seat and it took off speedily heading eastbound." She continued.

We have been continually in investigative mode of Louise Dipson, since. Later we arrested Antonio Calderon an accomplice of the perpetrator Louise Dipson. Our investigation also helped us to bring down other accomplices, Pimp Daddy and Sammy Grant.

Nine young teen girls were found murdered as a result of this alleged abduction serial spree.

Our first real encounter with Dipson began in a chase through Westchester County aborted in a road-kill accident. We were eluded by Louise Dipson after a multiple police car pile up. Days later she turned herself in at our South Bronx precinct."

Her partner Jonathan Hobbs corroborated her testimony.

35

As the trial continued, the McDonald's manager Arlene Gomez was put on the stand. During her cross-examination, the defense questioned: If Gomez was sure at that time of the evening and almost dark?

"How did you recognize the color of the getaway vehicle. It could have been black or dark gray."

To which Arlene Gomez responded:

"I know my colors. It was not black nor gray. It was midnight-blue. Here's a picture of the curb in the driveway that her vehicle grazed while she speedily tried to get away."

The picture was entered into evidence after matching up with an indentation on the SUV's photographic experiment.

Additionally, the experiment of the SUV was put up on the screen. Gomez assured the jury and the entire court that the vehicle in question was the getaway SUV.

The prosecution seemed as though they were in a rush to close the case. Weeping parents inside that SDNY courtroom anticipated a speedy climax. Pressure from the media, as well as those bereaved, was like a weight on the prosecution's back.

Additionally, Senators, Congressmen and other government officials were all applying pressure toward a swift verdict. It was like a stain on the judicial system as well as NYC. Most of those New York senator's seats remained vulnerable as the upcoming election was speedily approaching. Law enforcement was blamed for not doing enough to solve crime in the big city.

On the other hand, the prosecution could have called Sammy Grant to testify at this point and fulfilled the wish of the bereaved. Instead, they called Nikia Chavez the lone surviving victim. Nikia detailed she was about to visit the convenience store to buy groceries for her mother.

"The SUV pulled up as she crossed the street to enter. Louise Dipson was in the driver's seat. The rear door opened automatically.

Sammy Grant jumped out from the back seat. He put a bag over my head, one hand over my mouth, put my arm in a clinch behind my back and shoved me inside that SUV. He jumped in behind me. The door closed of its own accord and the thing drove off speedily. It seems like he was after me for years. I remembered him winking at me whenever our paths crossed at the local Post Office.

36

Inside the courtroom. You can hear a pin drop. Heads turned.

"What happened then?"

Asked Claudia Mendez for the prosecution.

"The SUV drove through the city streets and into some deserted areas. Grant kept touching me in private areas. Asked me if I'm a virgin? I told him I was. He told me he's a master at lovemaking. At this point, I felt cold sweats all over my body."

"What was the driver Louise Dipson doing at this point?"

Asked Mendez.

"She turned up the music loudly and continued speeding like a maniac."

Said Nikia.

"What else did Sammy Grant do?"

"He kept blowing into my left ear. I kept on resisting his advance. He asked me why I was trying to be a Little B... I told him I had a boyfriend."

"Tell me more. What else?"

Asked Prosecutor Mendez.

Louise Dipson pulled up on a side street filled with high shrubbery. She parked the SUV and attempted to get out. I yelled: Please don't do this to me! She proceeded anyway and slammed the door shut. He continued fondling me, removed my outer layers of clothing and raped me. He repeated himself multiple times: You were not a good girl and I'll give you a chance to redeem yourself tomorrow."

"What else?"

"He stuck an inhaler up my nose. That's the last thing I remembered."

"So, how did you wind up at the hotel?"

Asked Mendez.

Nikia broke down in tears.

"Not sure."

Said Nikia.

"When I woke up. I found myself tied up with rope to the bedframe in the hotel room."

Continued Nikia.

Did you know or ever met Cherae's mom Louise Dipson when you lived in Brooklyn and attended Crown Heights High?"

"Never did. But Cherry always bragged about her mother. Saying she's a born leader who's unstoppable and pushes her to succeed at astronomical levels."

"You mean Cherae."

"Yes. My friends and I called her Cherry because she dripped sweetness. Always such a giving person."

"What was she like on the court?"

Asked Claudia Mendez.

"Cherry was almost ungradable. She was our team's idol. Also, the idol of Crown Heights."

Says Nikia.

"Do you despise Sammy Grant now that you learned he was convicted and sentenced for taking Cherae Dipson's life?"

Asked the prosecution.

"You bet! I hate him!"

Responds Nikia.

She teared up once again. So did her mother sitting in that courtroom. Multiple jurors seemed locked into her story evident by their body language. Meanwhile, Louise Dipson remained poker-faced.

The Teen Advocate from the Williamsburg crime scene was seen taking copious notes inside that courtroom.

Once again Nikia welled up in tears and had to be aided off the witness stand and back to her seat.

Judge Thomas tactfully ordered a court recess. Which eventually materialized into a court adjournment until the next day.

37

The media went on a continued tirade overnight infused with talking points from Nikia Chavez's testimony.

Early the morning the defense began their cross of Nikia Chavez. They came at her with everything they could to benefit of their client Sammy Grant. Everything from that crack pipe found in her locker at school was thrown at her testimony. They labeled her as a crackpot and a blatant liar. Even asserting her trip to the grocery store could have been for the purchase of narc. As that locale was later closed by the Feds after a raid in which a huge volume of crack cocaine was seized.

"Why were you hanging out on that street?"

Questioned the defense. They even argued and doubted Nikia ever encountered Sammy Grant prior and even labeled her as a gold digger.

Nikia stuck to her testimony in an attempt to fend them off. Meanwhile, her mother in that courtroom could not stop her tear-flow.

Sammy Grant's defense questioned Louise Dipson's attitude through all this abduction. Trying to nail her to the cross intended for Sammy Grant. Nikia once again gave those vivid details of her abduction and rape as previously presented in her testimony to the prosecution.

Louise Dipson sitting in that courtroom yelled:

"Lying Bastard!" While Taliaferrow cross-examined Nkia Chavez.

The judge cautioned Dipson with a penalty for disrupting the court proceedings.

"Miss Dipson, if you are not willing to testify in your defense. I suggest you keep your comments to yourself. You can't have it both ways."

Dispson, in turn, held back her follow-up comment but later dropped underneath her breath.

" Lying Bastards!"

In the meantime, most of the jury engage in taking copious notes.

The defense pressed the teenager Nikia Chavez but was unable to punch any holes into her testimony. Leaving the prosecution team of Douglas Tibbs and Claudia Mendez in a feel-good situation regarding the testimony of their star witness.

38

Courtroom attendees by this time anticipated hearing from Pimp Daddy, Calderon, Sammy Grant, and of course Louise Dipson if she was going to testify. The defense, knowing Taliaferrow and Cochran could very much opt out of putting Dipson on the stand. While those thoughts simmered, the judge

126

called Pimp Daddy to the stand. Pimp Daddy took the oath. Feeling fresh from his testimony in the lawsuit against Sammy Grant.

Now like Déjà Vu both men implicated in this series of crimes orchestrated by Louise Dipson were back in the same courtroom together. Both stared each other down nefariously.

Sammy Grant already sentenced in the first case in which he raped and brutally murdered the daughter of Louise Dipson and Pimp Daddy still showed remorse. As most expected and debated, Pimp Daddy pleaded the fifth in this Louise Dipson trial. He no doubt wanted to remain loyal to Louise Dipson and reframed from implicating her. So, after taking the oath he torpedoed into that fifth dimension.

Will we hear from Calderon or not? This double-faced question not only sucked up the air in the courtroom but also in the media. A man senior in years and possessing enormous wealth would have much to say even though he previously pleaded the fifth. It seemed he wanted to walk back his decision to remain silent. Obviously, his cold feet stepped in. He felt it was way too much for him, as he shook nervously in his shoes inside the courtroom. Antonio Calderon eventually folded and returned to his seat. Leaving the impression that it would take a crowbar to shake lose whatever evidence he had in storage.

Next Sammy Grant was put on the hot seat. Getting a lighter sentence was foremost on his mind. He testified that he went along with the enterprise of Dipson, Calderon and Pimp Daddy just for the ride. As if the person who drives the getaway car is not complicit with the robbery.

Nikia Chavez had already pointed fingers at Sammy Grant as her abductor, who, raped and also threatened her life. It was apparent the quicksand was swaying quickly; Sammy Grant had no way of getting out of this swamp.

Ironically, his defense put up a strong case. Reasoning his client wanted nothing to do with the string of concentrated murders. However, he was dragged into it by Calderon, Dipson and Pimp Daddy.

The prosecution argued he was adept at what he did and when the opportunity presented itself again, he preyed on those innocent teen girls. He no doubt had to prove to himself and the world at large that he could engage in this kind of conduct and get away with it. If he didn't want to be part of ride why did he get on board?

39

In Dipson's defense, Samuel Taliaferrow pointed out that there was no evidence pointing her to the crime. Even the mid-night-blue SUV was registered to Calderon along with that mint green Land Rover. Plus, there was no DNA from Louise Dipson connected to any of the murdered victims. The only connect was to Nikia Chavez found on the ropes which were used to bind her.

The defense argued it was all hearsay. No one caught Dipson red-handed in any criminal activity. He also claimed his client was set up.

Additionally, when she saw how much damage Sammy Grant was causing to these young girls. She tied Nikia to the bedframe so Sammy Grant would not murder her in the woodlands. After which she turned herself in.

He also argued: Louise Dipson was never caught in the act and should not bear the penalty for someone else's crime.

On the other hand, the prosecution envisioned the maximum for Louise Dipson in this criminal conspiracy. Labeling her as the predator prove she was at the center of the operation.

"Her hands were dirty."

Said Claudia Mendez.

Also, the prosecution argued: Louise Dipson because of her termination from the department became bitter and created a vendetta which she harbored and would do anything to harm the NYPD. By taking them on a wild goose chase and exploiting their resources.

Louise Dipson led a street life and no doubt passed some of her street life down to her daughter Cherae. So, in order to drag the NYPD on the brink of sabotage and catastrophe she illegally wore their uniform to commit acts of murder against these innocent young teen girls. Using up taxpayers money for setting up roadblocks all over NYC to track her down.

40

Sammy Grant, on the other hand, saw profit and pleasure in her enterprise and bought in, lock, stock, and barrel. Bringing Calderon along for support. In this Calderon saw the opportunity to scar these young girls and collectively they exploited these 10 young teens girls.

Pimp daddy, settled in his enterprising ways could not keep bis hand out of the till. Wherever he saw greed and profit he latched on as his extended way of life.

Louise Dipson, Sammy Grant, Calderon, and Pimp Daddy deserve the maximum penalty allowed in New York State for their crimes. The jury would be doing less than they are capable and shirking their civic duty if they didn't find them guilty as charged.

The defense for Calderon and Sammy Grant argued their clients were coerced by Dipson and Pimp Daddy, and that they should be acquitted or given much lighter sentences for their crimes.

Meanwhile, Taliaferrow and Cochran tried to create sunlight between Antonio Calderon and Sammy Grant. They argued: Louise Dipson didn't have the heart to commit those murders. Despite everything, she had gone through. As a mother, no wonder she turned herself in, instead of inflicting any harm on Nikia Chavez. There comes a point in everyone's life when they must decide: If not me. Who? If not now, When? This ultimately happened for Louise Dipson. That's why she stood up for her daughter even after a two-year-old murder. I feel she could someday become a champion of reform. As a matter of fact, she has already begun the process in that direction.

After closing arguments, Judge Claude Thomas gaveled and sent the Jury to deliberate.

41

W hile the trial was underway. Louise Dipson and Pimp Daddy had been covertly attending Bible studies at a local church. The point came when then resolved to give their lives to Jesus Christ. However, the Pastor informed them that in order to get baptized it's a prerequisite for them to tie the knot.

Pimp Daddy was reluctant in getting married even if they had been together for years. Anyway, on a rainy Wednesday night in April, they were married in that neighborhood church. Witnesses to the event were Captain Jerome Meeks and Nicole Best-Meeks both recently married and members of that church assembly. It turned into a double event as the couple was baptized thereafter.

The jury deliberated for twelve days and finally returned verdicts:

Sammy Grant was found guilty for rape, aiding and abetting in a child abduction spree, and murdering seven young girls.

Calderon was found guilty of rape, aiding and abetting in a child abduction spree.

Pimp Daddy was found guilty in aiding and abetting in a child abduction spree.

Louise Dipson was found guilty of the attempted murder of Nikia Chavez and aiding and abetting in a child abduction spree.

All four defendants in this enterprise are awaiting sentencing in SDNY. Each crime committed was expected to carry a penalty of at least 15 years or more in prison.

About The Author

John A. Andrews, screenwriter, producer, playwright, director, and author of several books. As an author of almost 50 books in the genre on relationships, personal development, faith-based, and vivid engaging novels. Also, a playwright and screenwriter.

John is sought after as a motivational speaker to address success principles to young adults. He makes an impact in the lives of others because of his passion and commitment to make a difference in his life and the world.

Being a father of three sons propels John even more in his desire to see teens succeed. Andrews, a divorced dad of three sons Jonathan 24, Jefferri 22 and Jamison 19. Andrews was born in the Islands of St. Vincent and the Grenadines. His two eldest sons are also writers and wrote their first two novels while teenagers.

Andrews grew up in a home of five sisters and three brothers. He recounts: "My parents were all about values: work hard, love God and never give up on your dreams."

Self-educated, John developed an interest in music. Although lacking formal education, he later put his knowledge and passion to good use, moonlighting as a disc jockey in New York. This paved the way for further exploration in the world of entertainment. In 1994 John caught the acting bug. Leaving the Big Apple for Hollywood over a decade ago not only put several national TV commercials under his belt but helped him to find his niche. He also appeared in the movie John Q starring Denzel Washington.

His passion for writing started in 2002 when he was denied the rights to a 1970's classic film, which he so badly wanted to remake. In 2007, while etching two of his original screenplays, he published his first book "The 5 Steps to Changing Your Life"

In 2008 he not only published his second book but also wrote 7 additional books that year, and produced the docu-drama based on his second book; *Spread Some Love (Relationships 101).*

137

Currently, he just published book 47 and working on 48, 49 and 50. With several in the movie and TV pipeline.

See Imdb: http://www.imdb.com/title/tt0854677/.

FOR MORE ON

BOOKS THAT WILL ENHANCE YOUR LIFE ™

Visit: **A L I**

www.JohnAAndrews.com

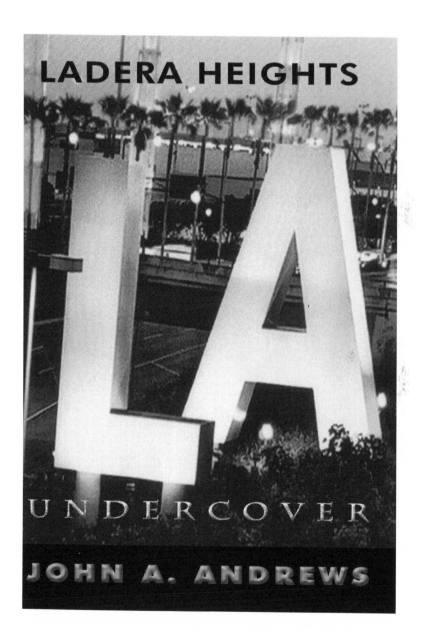

DESIREE O'GARRO

THE LETHAL KID

A TEEN THRILLER

FROM THE CREATORS OF

RUDE BUAY
AGENT O'GARRO
RENEGADE COPS
A SNITCH ON TIME
WHO SHOT THE SHERIFF?
&
*THE MACOS ADVENTURE

#1 INTERNATIONAL BESTSELLING AUTHOR

JOHN A. ANDREWS
&
·JEFFERRI ANDREWS

NEW
RELEASES

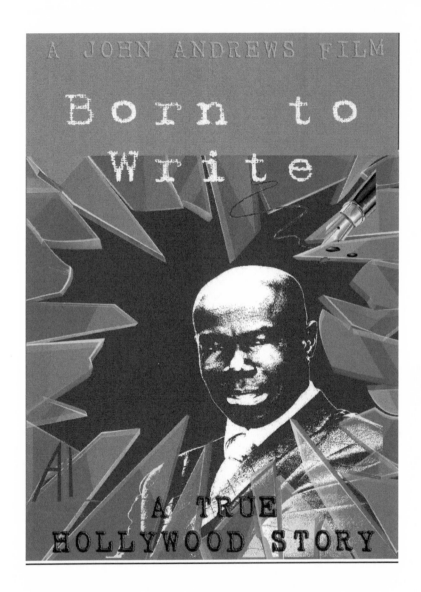

NEW YORK CONNIVERS ©

FROM THE CREATOR OF *WHO SHOT THE SHERIFF?*

JOHN A. ANDREWS

UNTIL DEATH DO US PART

A NOVEL

ONE FOOT IN *NEW YORK UNDERCOVER*
THE OTHER IN *ALFRED HITCHCOCK PRESENTS*

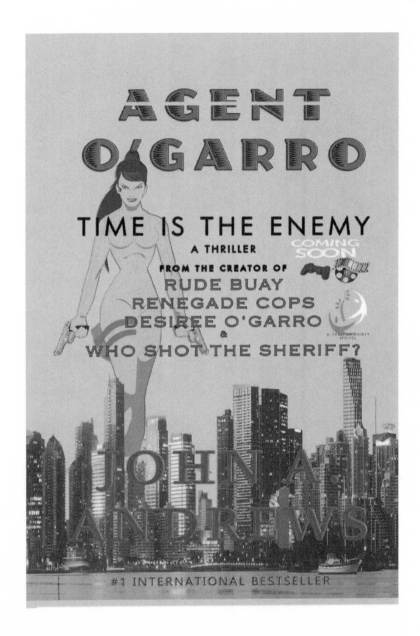

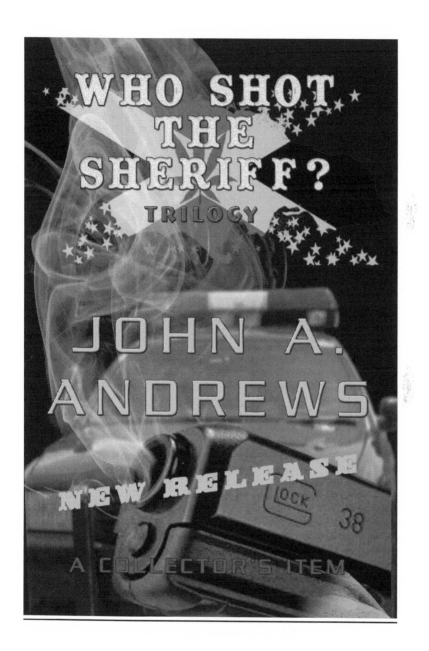

<u>OTHER RELEASES</u>

National Bestselling Author of
Rude Buay ... The Unstoppable

THE 5
STEPS TO
CHANGING
YOUR LIFE
BY: JOHN A. ANDREWS

JOHN A. ANDREWS

THE MUSICAL°

FROM THE CREATOR OF
RUDE BUAY
THE WHODUNIT CHRONICLES
&
THE CHURCH ON FIRE

SO MANY ARE TRYING TO GO TO HEAVEN
WITHOUT FIRST BUILDING A HEAVEN
HERE ON EARTH...
#1 INTERNATIONAL BESTSELLER

THAT CONNECTS
PRAISE
HEAVEN & EARTH•

JOHN A. ANDREWS
CREATOR OF:
THE CHURCH ... A HOSPITAAL?
&
THE CHURCH ON FIRE

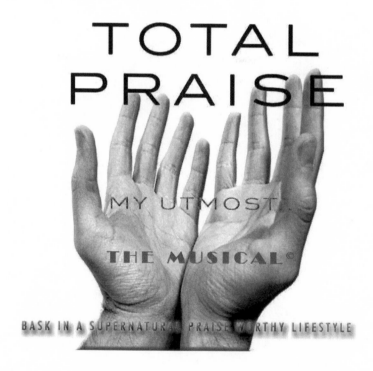

TOTAL
PRAISE

MY UTMOST...

THE MUSICAL©

BASK IN A SUPERNATURAL PRAISEWORTHY LIFESTYLE

COMING ON SUNDAYS
2019 TBA
THAT CONNECTS
PRAISE
HEAVEN & EARTH

THE
CHURCH
ON FIRE
THE MUSICAL®
WRITTEN & DIRECTED BY JOHN A. ANDREWS

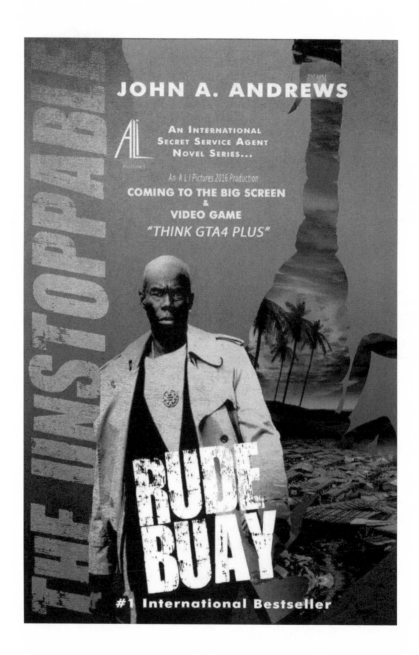

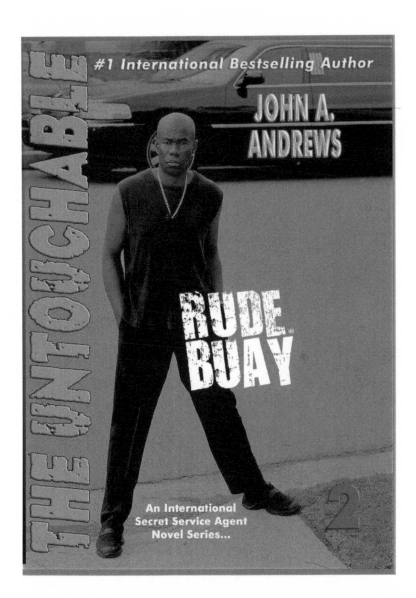

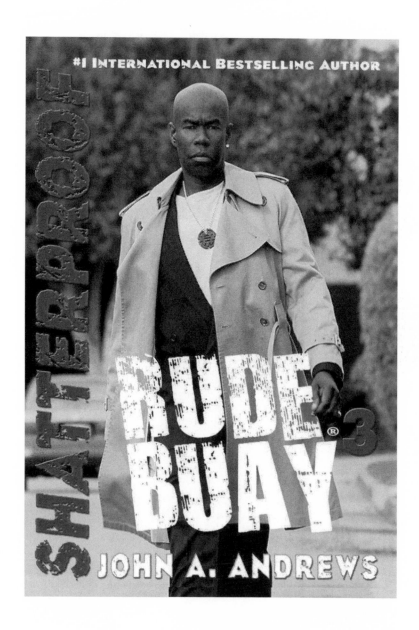

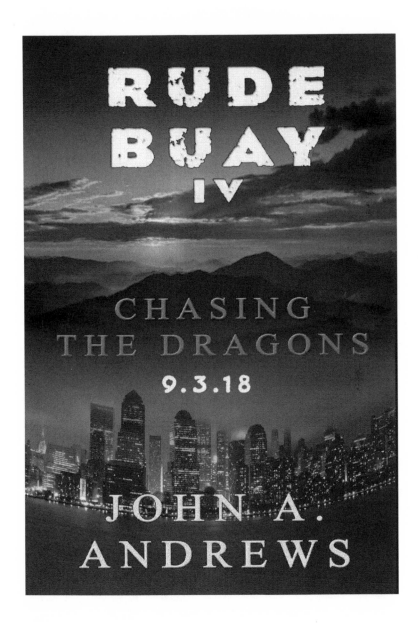

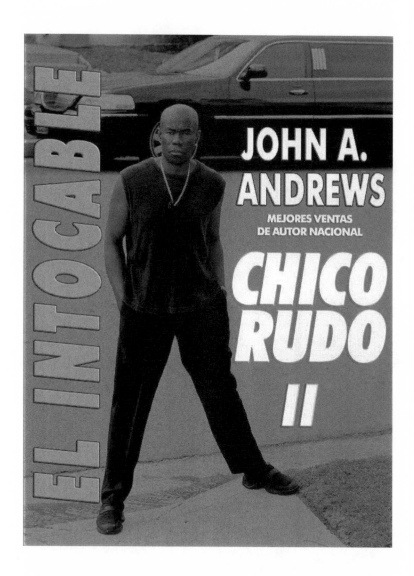

CROSS ATLANTIC FIASCO

BLOOD IS THICKER THAN WATER

JOHN A. ANDREWS

Creator of
The RUDE BUAY Series

~ A Novel ~

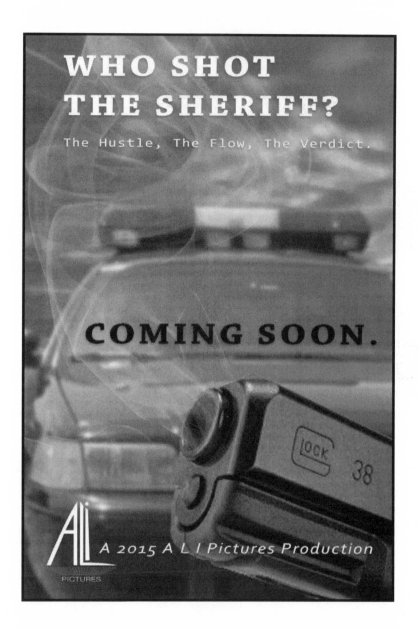

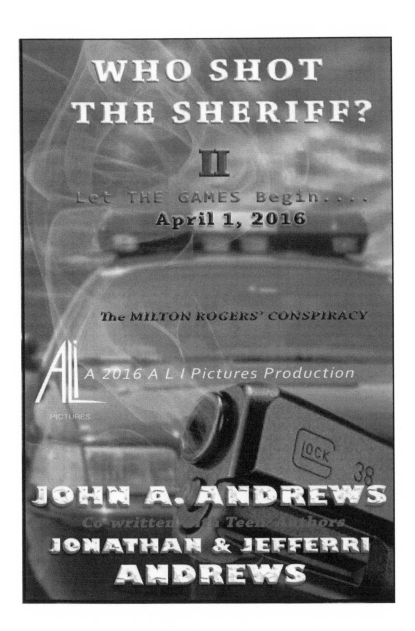

THE AUTHORITY SQUAD
THE MACOS ADVENTURE
2
A TEEN NOVEL
JONATHAN
&
JEFFERRI ANDREWS
With
International Bestselling Author
JOHN A. ANDREWS

LOUISE DIPSON (THE PREDATOR)

VISIT: WWW.JOHNAANDREWS.COM

UNCANNY PICTURES